The *Very* Fairy Princess
Graduation Girl!

by Julie Andrews & Emma Walton Hamilton

Illustrated by
Christine Davenier

Little, Brown and Company
New York   Boston

Hello, hello!

I'm Gerry! I'm a very fairy princess.

Not everyone believes me, and I try not to brag about it too much.

(But my wings and crown do give me away a bit.)

Fairy princesses are VERY enthusiastic.
We love being creative and hobnobbing
with new friends, and we're at our BEST
on special occasions.
It's the perfect way to share
our SPARKLE with the world!

Speaking of special occasions, a BIG one is around the corner.

It's the end of the school year...GRADUATION TIME!

We've returned all our library books, finished our special projects,
and emptied our cubbies.

Next year, we'll be in a NEW classroom with a NEW teacher.

To be honest, I'm having a hard time finding my sparkle about this.

(Change is HARD...even for a fairy princess.)

First of all, I LOVE Miss Pym, the teacher we've had all year.
She lets me wear my crown in class, and we get to paint and dance
and sing and do fun projects.

I also love our classroom and our class pet, Houdini the hamster.
Miss Pym says my "exuberance" will set the tone wherever I go,
and we are ALL ready to move on.

I don't feel ready at all!
We don't even know who
the new teacher will be.

Miss Pym says she's sure it will be someone
very nice. How can she be so sure?
What if it's a grumpy witch with a wart on her nose?

What if there's no class pet?

Worst of all, what if I'm not allowed to bring my wings and crown to class?

(Fairy princesses are team players, but it's important to be ready for curveballs.)

Mommy says she's sure everything will be just fine,
and besides, all my friends are moving up as well.
Daddy says my sparkle will brighten ANY classroom.

My brother, Stewart, says I'd be a princess
even if I wore a paper bag on my head.
This does NOT help.

On the last day of school,
things get even WORSE.
All our artwork comes down off the walls—
even my life-size portrait of Miss Pym.
We say good-bye to Houdini, who is going
to a farm for summer vacation.

The classroom looks SO empty.

I'm going to miss everything SO much!

(Fairy princesses can be a tad sentimental.)

Miss Pym gathers us together on the rug.
"Good news, boys and girls!" she says.
"Your new teacher has been announced.
His name is Mr. Bonario."
MISTER Bonario?

Our new teacher is a MAN?

He'll NEVER believe that I'm a fairy princess!

And he can't POSSIBLY appreciate my wings and crown!

This is going to be the most UN-sparkly year in school history!

The next morning, I am SO upset I can hardly eat breakfast.
Daddy makes his special pancakes, but I only have three.
(Even a fairy princess can lose her appetite when she's stressed.)

Mommy tells me I have the whole summer to get used
to the idea of a new teacher.
I say, "Well, I don't want him calling me GERALDINE!"
Stewart says, "Oh, puh-leeze!"

When I get to school, there is ANOTHER problem.
We have to wear a funny hat with a tassel and a blue robe for graduation.
I can go without my wings for the ceremony,
but I can't POSSIBLY give up my crown!
(A fairy princess without a crown is like a cone without ice cream!)

Miss Pym understands.

She pins my crown on top of my hat.

"Congratulations, my fairy princess graduate," she says.

"Keep that sparkle bright!"

The hat feels wobbly, so I walk with my head very straight.
(Fairy princesses have PERFECT posture, so it's easy to adjust.)

The graduation ceremony begins.
Miss Pym and some of the other
teachers make speeches, telling our
parents how proud they are of us.
Mr. Higginbottom leads us all in a song.

Then our names are called, and one by one we walk
through the graduation arch.
Everyone applauds, and we throw our hats in the air.
WHEEE!

OH NO! My CROWN!
It flies off my hat and
sails over the audience.

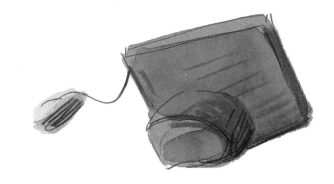

A hand reaches up to snatch it.

Whose can it be?

Will I ever get my crown back?

Graduation is RUINED!

After the ceremony, there's a party
with cupcakes and punch,
but I'm too upset to celebrate.
I am putting my wings back on
when a voice says,
"I think this belongs to you?"

A man with curly hair
and twinkly eyes
is holding my crown!
He has orange sneakers
and polka-dotted socks.

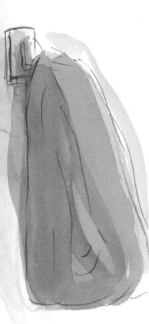

"A fairy princess should never be
without her royal accessories,"
he says, smiling.
"Gerry, isn't it? I'm Mr. Bonario.
I'm SO happy you'll be in my class.
You're going to love Hazel,
our pet hedgehog!"

Looks like next year will be SUPER-sparkly after all!

For all the dedicated teachers who make a difference.

—J.A. & E.W.H.

*To Edmund White, my dear friend who invited me to stay with him in
Providence and changed my life!*

—C.D.

The illustrations for this book were done in ink and color pencil on Kaecolor paper.

The text was set in Baskerville and the display type is Mayfair.

This book was edited by Liza Baker and designed by Phil Caminiti with art direction by Patti Ann Harris.

The production was supervised by Erika Schwartz, and the production editor was Christine Ma.

Text copyright © 2014 by Julie Andrews Edwards Trust—1989 and Beech Tree Books, LLC • Illustrations copyright © 2014 by Christine Davenier • All rights reserved. In accordance with the U.S. Copyright Act of 1976, the scanning, uploading, and electronic sharing of any part of this book without the permission of the publisher is unlawful piracy and theft of the author's intellectual property. If you would like to use material from the book (other than for review purposes), prior written permission must be obtained by contacting the publisher at permissions@hbgusa.com. Thank you for your support of the author's rights. • Little, Brown and Company • Hachette Book Group • 237 Park Avenue, New York, NY 10017 • Visit our website at www.lb-kids.com • Little, Brown and Company is a division of Hachette Book Group, Inc. • The Little, Brown name and logo are trademarks of Hachette Book Group, Inc. • The publisher is not responsible for websites (or their content) that are not owned by the publisher. • First Edition: April 2014 • Library of Congress Cataloging-in-Publication Data • Andrews, Julie. • The Very Fairy Princess: graduation girl! / by Julie Andrews & Emma Walton Hamilton ; illustrated by Christine Davenier.—First edition. • pages cm • Summary: As the school year draws to an end, Gerry has a hard time finding her sparkle knowing that she will say goodbye to her teacher, Miss Pym, and class pet Houdini, and start anew in a classroom where she may not be recognized as a very fairy princess. • ISBN 978-0-316-21960-0 [1. Change—Fiction. 2. Teachers—Fiction. 3. Schools—Fiction. 4. Princesses—Fiction.] I. Hamilton, Emma Walton. II. Davenier, Christine, illustrator. III. Title. • PZ7.A5673Vgm 2014 • [E]—dc23 • 2013014112 • 10 9 8 7 6 5 4 3 2 1 • SC • Printed in China